ONE
DOZEN BROWNIES

by Anne Guy

illustrated by Gloria Kamen

New York ABINGDON PRESS Nashville

To the children, parents,
and faculty,
of Chevy Chase
Elementary School,
In appreciation of their
loyal affection

CONTENTS

1.

ABOUT BIRTHDAYS AND BROWNIES

Karen Grant was walking home with her very best friend, Barbara Baker.

"Tomorrow is my birthday," she said. "I will be eight years old tomorrow."

"Everybody in third grade knows that," said Barbara. "You've reminded Miss Shay about it every day for a year."

"Oh, not a year, Babs," protested Karen. "I only told her two or three times."

"Too bad you can't have a birthday party," said Babs reaching down to pick up a bright pink stone.

"But who would come if I had a party, Babs?

All the girls I know are going to Brownie meeting after school tomorrow. Except you. And you have riding lessons."

Babs' cheerful freckled face changed. She frowned and began to chew the end of one of her short red braids.

"Miss Shay called my mom up last night," she said. "Miss Shay is going to be assistant leader to the Brownies and guess what? She wants my mom to be troop leader."

"I know," said Karen. "Miss Shay told us."

"If my mom is troop leader, I'll have to be a Brownie. And then I won't be able to ride on Tuesdays. I think Miss Shay is mean to want my mom to be leader."

"Oh, Babs, she is not," cried Karen. "She's the nicest teacher in the whole school."

"Well, I'd much rather ride a horse than go to any old Brownie meeting," said Babs angrily.

The girls walked along in silence for a few minutes. Karen was thinking about her birthday again.

"Even if I wasn't going to Brownie meeting, how could I have a party?" she asked after a while. "My mother doesn't even get home from work until

five o'clock. And besides, it's Pooky's birthday, too. He will be three."

"Well, you'd have Pooky at your party then," said Babs, with a giggle.

"That's just the trouble!" Karen groaned. "Mother always makes us have our birthdays together. Pooky spoils everything. I never even get a birthday cake all my own. Why do I have to have a little brother, anyway?"

"I feel the same way," agreed Babs cheerfully. "My big sister Andrea is so stuck up, she makes me sick."

"We think the same most of the time," said

7

Karen. "Won't you change your mind about Brownies, Babs? It's going to be fun to have a club like our mothers have—with refreshments and everything. Please decide to be a Brownie."

The girls came to the corner where they always parted. It was halfway between their two homes. Babs always walked that far with Karen, then ran back up the hill to her own house.

"I'll be glad if you give up your riding lessons," went on Karen. "Then you won't be always going to library or bookmobile for horse books. And we can be together more. Call me up tonight and let me know what your mom says."

Babs turned to run up the hill. She looked back at Karen.

"K.O.," she shouted, waving. "Ees - u."

Karen giggled. She and Babs said words backwards whenever they wanted to talk to each other in secret language.

"Ees - u," shouted Karen, waving back.

And she hummed a little tune as she went hippity hopping home.

2.

ONE DOZEN BROWNIES

Karen could hardly wait to get to school the next morning.

"I'm eight years old today. I'm going to Brownie meeting at half past three this afternoon," she told herself. "Oh, what an exciting day! If only Babs will decide to go, too."

Just then Karen caught sight of Babs running toward her down the hill. As Babs came closer, Karen could see that her cheeks were streaked with tears and her face was red and angry.

"I'm going to hate Brownies. I know I am," Babs sobbed, as the two girls met.

"Are you going to be one, Babs?" asked Karen eagerly. "Why didn't you call me up last night?"

"It was Andrea's fault," said Babs. "My mom talked and talked to me until it was too late to call you. Mom says Andrea is going to college. And college costs a lot of money. And riding lessons cost money. Andrea needs my riding money for college. It's not fair. My horse lessons are just as important as Andrea's old college is."

Karen gave a little skip of happiness. "Oh, Babs, then you are going to be a Brownie! Oh, I'm so glad. What do you care about smelly old horses? Now you can walk to Brownies with me every Tuesday. That's much more fun."

Babs gave an angry sniff.

"That's all you know about horses, Karen Grant," she said. "Horses are not smelly! And walking to Brownie meeting isn't going to be one bit of fun."

She wiped her eyes on her sleeve as the bell rang, and the two girls hurried into the school building.

That afternoon Babs was the last of the twelve girls to come out the back door of the school. She

10

did not join the others as they laughed and talked, waiting for Miss Shay.

"Come here and stand by me, Babs," shouted Karen as Miss Shay came hurrying out.

"Are we all here?" Miss Shay asked. "Line up girls, all twelve of you. One dozen Brownies. I'll have to call our troop my Brownie Dozen."

"I like that name," laughed Karen. She slipped her hand into her teacher's. "May Babs and I walk with you, Miss Shay?"

A fat little girl with black bobbed hair and flashing black eyes gave her a shove.

"Me first," she shouted. "I have to show the way because Brownie meetings are going to be in our new house. Just wait till you see the rec room, Miss Shay. It's so big that we can keep all our things there."

Karen fell back and slipped her arm through Babs', as they all started down the street.

"That bossy Jane Foster," she whispered. "I'd rather walk with you than anyone else anyway—even Miss Shay."

Babs did not reply. But she smiled at Karen and squeezed her hand.

Soon they reached Jane's new home, a large brick house. Mrs. Baker was waiting at the recreation room door to greet them. She showed them where to put their wraps. Then all the girls sat down on the floor in a circle.

"What would you like to know first about being Brownies, girls?" Mrs. Baker asked.

"When can we get our uniforms and wear them?" asked Susie, a pale, timid-looking little girl, with soft blue eyes and big glasses.

"Not until the fifth meeting," said Mrs. Baker.

"Oh," said Susie with a disappointed look, "why do we have to wait so long? How can we be real Brownies without wearing uniforms?"

"It is not the uniform that makes you a Brownie, Susie. It's learning the Brownie Promise and the Salute and how to help others. When you have

13

learned these things, you will be invested. Then you can wear a uniform. That will be at the fifth meeting."

The Brownies all sat quiet for a minute, thinking about this.

Then Jane demanded, "Well, when do we choose a president for this club? I think I should be president, since this is my house."

Babs spoke up quickly. "My mother is the troop leader, Jane Foster. So I should be president."

"I choose Babs," shouted Karen. "Babs should be president."

"Girls, girls," laughed Mrs. Baker. "That is not the way Brownies choose a president. Brownies vote for president, just the way your daddy and mother vote for President of the United States." Jane scowled, and Babs chewed her red braid.

"You don't need a president yet anyway," went on Mrs. Baker. "But you do need a hostess. The hostess is always the daughter of the mother who sends the refreshments for the meeting."

The girls looked at each other. Had anyone brought refreshments? Had all the mothers forgotten?

14

Mrs. Baker smiled.

"Miss Shay brought refreshments this time. So she'll have to choose the hostess."

"Me—me—choose me," they all shouted at once.

Karen wished Miss Shay would choose her. After all it was her birthday! But Miss Shay didn't even look at Karen.

"I choose Susie," she said.

"Let's eat right now, can't we, Mrs. Baker?" asked Jane. "Let's have refreshments. I'm hungry."

"Not quite yet," laughed Mrs. Baker. "First we must decide what our first project will be and learn the Brownie Promise and Salute. Come, let's stand up. I'll show you the Salute. Then you may say the Promise after me. It goes like this——

"I promise to do my best, to love God and my country, to help people every day, especially those at home."

3.

THE GIRL NEXT DOOR

The girls soon learned the Salute, the Greeting Sign, and the Handshake. They ran all over the big rec room, shaking hands and greeting each other.

"Ouch," shouted Jane. "Babs always squeezes hands too tight."

They decided that their first project would be to fix up the big rec room and make tables and curtains and sit-up-ons. And then they put on their coats and dashed out into the back yard for a game.

"Play a circle game," called Mrs. Baker. "Don't

get on Mrs. Foster's flower beds or fall into the pool. Susie will stay here and help us."

"Let's play Go in and Out the Windows," shouted Jane.

"No, Pop Goes the Weasel! It's more fun," cried Karen.

Just as they were making a circle, Karen noticed something. "Look," she said softly, pointing.

There, in the sunshine, in the big yard next door, was a wheel chair. In it, bundled with blankets, was a girl. She looked pale and sick.

"We haven't lived here long enough to meet our neighbors yet," whispered Jane. "All the houses are new. I didn't know there was a girl next door. I wonder what's the matter with her."

"Maybe she had her tonsils out and just came home from the hospital," said Karen.

"Well, don't just stare at her," said Babs. "Come on. Let's play. I vote for Karen's game first, and then we'll play yours, Jane."

But Karen couldn't forget the girl next door.

She saw that the girl was pretending not to watch but that she couldn't help getting a little excited over all the fun they were having. When Susie

called them in for refreshments, Karen stayed behind, hoping she might go over and talk to her.
But the girl had turned her face away.

Karen was the last one to go back into the rec
room. She hurried in, afraid she was late for refreshments. But the girls were all waiting for her.

"Happy Birthday, Karen," they screamed. And
there on a little table in the center of the room was
a beautiful pink cake. And on it were eight pink
candles.

Miss Shay smiled at Karen's surprise.

"We don't usually celebrate the girls' birthdays at Brownie meetings, Karen," she said. "But because you have always wanted a birthday cake all your own, Mrs. Baker and I decided we would celebrate this once."

"Oh, Miss Shay," cried Karen, her eyes shining. "I just love being a Brownie."

"Well," said Miss Shay, "make a wish and blow out your candles, and then you may help Susie pass your cake."

Karen flew about the room as if on wings.

"Just exactly fourteen pieces," she said, helping herself to the last piece on the plate. "You pass the punch, Susie. I can't wait any longer to eat my cake."

She opened her mouth to take a big bite. Then she stopped and put the piece back on the plate.

Running to Miss Shay, she whispered something in her teacher's ear.

"I think that is a nice idea," Miss Shay said smiling. She helped Karen cut her piece of cake carefully in half and wrap one part of it in a paper napkin.

Before even Babs had noticed, Karen skipped

out the door. She was back in a few minutes, her eyes shining and both her dimples showing.

"Well, Karen, where have you been?" demanded Jane curiously.

"Next door," said Karen happily. "The sick girl's name is Holly. She is eight years old. Something is the matter with her leg. She can't walk." And Karen took a big bite of her very own birthday cake as Susie handed her a glass of pink punch.

4.

WISHES

It was Saturday morning.

Karen was drying the dishes for her mother. Her little brother, Pooky, sat on the kitchen floor, playing with his blocks.

Mrs. Grant was dressed for work. She had her hat on and a pretty white apron tied around her waist.

"You look very nice this morning, Mrs. Grant," said Karen, looking at her mother with loving eyes.

Mrs. Grant laughed.

"Thank you, chick-a-biddy," she said.

Karen's father was dead. He had died just after

Pooky was born, and Mrs. Grant had to go to work. She often worked on Saturdays.

"Be sure and get home this afternoon to help Mrs. Apple with Pooky," said Mrs. Grant. "Be home by two o'clock."

Mrs. Apple was the baby sitter who came every day while Karen's mother was away.

"Oh, Mom," Karen cried frowning. "Babs asked me to have lunch and stay all day with her. Why do I have to come home? Why can't you be like other mothers and stay home and take care of Pooky and me yourself?"

Mrs. Grant put down the cup she was holding. She put her hands on her daughter's shoulders and looked at her seriously.

"You know why," she said. She pointed to a big piece of paper that Karen had put on the kitchen wall. It had a picture of a Brownie trefoil drawn at the top. In big letters Karen had printed

A BROWNIE IN THIS HOUSE COULD
1. Help with the dishes
2. Set the table
3. Make her own bed

"I can think of a fourth thing you might write
on that paper before you take it to the next
Brownie meeting," said Mother.

Just then the phone rang.

It was Babs.

"Hi, Babs," shouted Karen.

"Downtown?"

"Oh, you lucky!"

"Wait, I'll ask Mom."

She turned to her mother.

"Mrs. Baker is going to take Babs downtown to get her Brownie uniform this afternoon. She says I may go along. Can I get mine, too? Oh, please Mom, can I?"

"I'm sorry, Karen," said Mrs. Grant. "You will be needed here with Pooky. And besides, you won't have to have a uniform for two more weeks."

Karen put down the receiver, tears in her eyes.

"Well, here comes that old Mrs. Apple up the walk," she said. "And I'm going to Babs' house right this minute where people have fun and don't have to work all the time."

She banged the door and ran across the lawn without even a hello to Mrs. Apple or a good-by to Pooky and Mother.

She passed Jane's house, but no one was about.

Probably her mother has taken her somewhere that is fun, she thought gloomily.

Then she caught a glimpse of something pink. It was Holly, sitting in the sunshine.

Rather timidly, Karen walked around the house to where Holly sat.

"Hi," she said.

Holly smiled.

"Hi, Karen," she answered.

"Where have you been the last two Brownie meetings?" asked Karen curiously. "You weren't in the yard and your house was all shut up tight. I looked for you."

Holly leaned back against her pillow.

"I had to go to the hospital again," she said. "But I'm glad you looked for me. Did you have fun at the Brownie meetings?"

Karen's face lighted.

She dropped down on the grass at Holly's feet.

"Oh, it was super, Holly. We made sit-up-ons for the rec room out of oilcloth. Jane's father came and helped us make tables and chairs out of boxes from the supermarket, and Mrs. Baker helped us cut some flowered goods for our curtains. We are going to begin sewing at our next meeting."

"Oh, I just love to sew," Holly said.

"Well, I don't," said Karen. "I hate it. I wish you were a Brownie, Holly, so you could show me how to do my sewing. Maybe I'd let you do it for me," she said giggling.

"Oh, I wish I could be a Brownie. I'd love to be a Brownie more than anything else I know of," said Holly wistfully. "But I don't suppose I can until I can walk again and go to school; and that will be a long time, the doctor says."

Karen reached over and squeezed Holly's hand.

"I wish I were a fairy princess," she said. "I'd wave my magic wand over you and you'd jump right out of the chair and dance with me right now. Do you like fairy stories, Holly?"

"Oh yes," said Holly.

"Well, you should read *The Brownie Story* then," said Karen. "It's by Julianna Ewing. I can get it at the library for you. Miss Shay told it to us at Brownie meeting and guess what, we are going to act it out for Investiture. I can hardly wait. I hope I'll get chosen to be Mary."

"Oh, Karen, tell me the story. Are Brownies fairies?"

"Well, people in Scotland used to believe there were little elves or fairies called Brownies," said Karen.

Then she told Holly the story.

5.

THE BROWNIE STORY

There was a little girl named Mary. Her brother was Tommy. They lived in Scotland with their grandmother and their father, who was a tailor.

They were all very poor. The grandmother and the father had to work hard. But Mary and Tommy didn't want to do any work. They didn't like to help at home.

"Children are a burden," said the poor tailor.

Only he called the children "bairns" because "bairns" is the way Scotch people say children.

"Bairns are a burden," he said.

"Oh, no," said the grandmother. "Bairns are not a burden. Bairns are a blessing."

One day Grandmother told Mary a story. It was a story about a little fairy brownie who lived with Grandmother when she was a little girl.

"A Brownie lived at our house for years and years," Grandmother said. "She would get up each morning and sweep the floor and set the breakfast table and do all the work. And then she would run off before anyone could catch her.

"How did you know it was a Brownie who did the work?" asked Mary.

"Oh, we could hear her laugh and play as she worked."

"Did you pay her any wages?"

"Oh, my, no. A Brownie works for love. We would leave her a bowl of clear water or a bowl of cream sometimes. But she went away one day and never came back and the luck of our house went with her."

"Why did she go away?" Mary asked.

"Only the wise old hoot owl who lives in the woods can answer that question," said Grandmother.

"Well," said Mary. "I think I'll go and see if I can find that old hoot owl. I'll get the Brownie to come back and keep our house and run our errands for us."

So one night when there was a big silver moon in the sky and white, silvery moonlight lay over everything, Mary went into the forest.

"Hoot, hoot," said a voice behind her.

There was Old Owl, up in a tree.

"Please tell me how to find a Brownie who will come and live at our house and help us with the work," said Mary.

"Oo—who—oo," said the owl. "Two Brownies live at your house right now. But they are lazy. They do not like to work."

"If you will tell me where I can find the two Brownies," said Mary, "I will talk to them and tell them what work to do. There is such a lot of work to do at our house."

"I can tell you where to go to find one of the Brownies," said Old Owl. "Listen—

"When the moon is shining, go to a pool and turn yourself about three times. Then say this charm.

30

"Twist me and turn me
And show me the Elf,
I looked in the water
And saw —"
"Will I see a Brownie?" asked Mary.
"You must think of a word that rhymes with

Elf," said Old Owl. "And then say the word if you do see a Brownie."

"But what if I don't see a Brownie?"

"Then it is no use to answer," said Old Owl.

"Well, the moon is shining right now. So here I go. Thank you, Old Owl," said Mary. And off she went to the pool.

She looked down into the dark water. She turned herself slowly around and said the magic words.

"Twist me and turn me
And show me the Elf,
I looked in the water
And saw ——"

She bent over and looked deep in the water, but not a thing did she see but her own face looking up.

"Kelf, pelf, helf," she said. "What is the magic word?"

"I must have done it wrong. There is no one there but myself. Self—why that rhymes with elf. But there is no Brownie there. The charm did not work."

So back she went to Old Owl.

"Who—who—who—did you see?"

"Only myself," said Mary. "I wanted to see a Brownie. I'm not a Brownie."

"Did you find a rhyming word?"

"No," said Mary. "No word but myself."

"Well, that rhymes," said Old Owl. "Don't you know that all children can be Brownies if they wish? But they must learn to be useful and helpful and to work."

"Well, I don't like to work," said Mary.

"Oh, you would rather be lazy and idle, is that it?" asked Old Owl.

"No, I don't really want to be lazy," said Mary. "I want to be helpful."

"Good," said Old Owl. "Then go and find your brother and tell him all about what happened. But remember, good deeds are better done in secret. Brownies are never seen at their work."

So Mary and Tommy worked out a plan. The very next morning they got up before the old folks. They swept and dusted the house and started breakfast and made the fire.

When the poor tailor came downstairs, he was surprised. He thought the Brownie had come back.

"Our luck has changed," he told Grandmother.

Everyone in the house became happy, and the house was full of laughter. Each day Mary and Tommy found more and more things to do, and they were the happiest of all.

Then one morning the tailor stole downstairs to watch for the Brownie and see how it could be possible for one little Brownie to do so many nice things.

And there he saw Mary and Tommy laughing and singing and doing all the work.

"What's this? Where is the Brownie?" he asked.

"We are the Brownie," said the children.

"Stop fooling! Where is the real Brownie?"

"We are the only Brownie there is," said Mary.

"But who did all the work around the house every day?" asked the tailor.

"We did, all of it."

"Well," said the tailor to the old grandmother, who had come into the room, too. "What do you think of all this?"

"I think bairns are a blessing," said the old woman. "I told you they were."

"Oh, what a lovely story," said Holly. "How I wish I could work and help around the house."

"Won't you be well soon?" asked Karen. "Can't you get out of your wheel chair? Can't you walk?"

"The doctor says I should try to walk. But I'm afraid. It hurts. It's too hard."

"Oh, Holly," begged Karen. "Do try."

Just then someone came roller skating up the walk. It was Babs. She looked cross.

"Where have you been, Karen Grant? I've been looking everywhere for you."

"Ooops," said Karen, jumping up, "I did start for your house, Babs."

"Well, are you coming to my house or not, Miss Karen Grant? You don't have to come, if you don't want to."

"I'll be over in two shakes, Babs, but I've got to go home a minute first."

"What for?" asked Babs. "I'll go with you."

"No, it's a secret," cried Karen, and before Babs or Holly could say another word, she ran off.

"Mrs. Apple—Mrs. Apple," she shouted running in the kitchen and grabbing her around the waist.

"I just thought I'd tell you I'll be home at two o'clock to help with Pooky."

"Sakes alive," said Mrs. Apple. "Why of course you will. I told your mother I knew you'd come."

Karen ran over to the kitchen wall. She picked up a brown crayon and printed carefully.

4. Helps take care of little brother

"Pooky, you're a bairn," she said.

Pooky looked up, his eyes big and round.

"Yes," he said. "I'm a bear—a big black bear!"

"Not a bear, a bairn," said Karen. "And I'm a Brownie, and Mrs. Apple is the old hoot owl."

And banging the door behind her, she was off to have lunch with Babs.

6.

"TWIST ME AND TURN ME"

Babs Baker came running across the lawn of Mrs. Foster's back yard. She rushed over to the wheel chair where Holly Hillman sat. Karen stood beside her.

"Guess what," shouted Babs.

"Well, what?" asked Karen, twirling the skirt of her new Brownie uniform.

"Susie just said she won't be the owl," announced Babs.

The two girls looked at Babs in dismay.

"Susie's front tooth fell out in school today," Babs went on. "We all saw it fall out. But now

Susie says the mothers will see that her tooth is out and they won't think she looks like an owl. She says to tell Holly just to read her part."

"Oh, no," said Holly, looking down at a book on her lap. "I don't believe I'm going to read the story at all. I might make mistakes, and I might not read loud enough. And besides, I'm not even a Brownie."

"But all the Brownies wanted you to read it, Holly. Oh, please do read, Holly—please do," begged Karen.

She looked so worried that Holly thought again.

"Well, O.K.," she said at last, and Karen threw both arms around her in a big hug.

"I love you, Holly," she cried. "Babs, you go right back to Susie and tell her she's just got to be the owl. She'll look more like an owl with her tooth out because owls don't show their teeth to everybody. Go tell her quick."

As Babs raced off to find Susie, Karen turned to Holly again. "Isn't everything exciting today? Only I wish my mother could have come."

Just then Mrs. Baker came over. She pushed Holly's chair to the center of the yard and held up two fingers. This was the Brownie signal that meant silence, and everyone got quiet.

"It is so nice to have the mothers here on this very special afternoon," said Mrs. Baker. "Please come up a little closer so that you can see and hear the play the girls have prepared for you. They are going to pantomime a part of *The Brownie Story*. Holly Hillman will read it. Karen Grant is Mary. Babs Baker is the grandmother. Jane Foster is the tailor, and Susie Wells is the owl."

"Ooops!" cried Karen, suddenly putting both hands over her mouth. "Where's the rocking chair? Babs forgot her rocking chair."

Just then the door of the rec room opened and Miss Shay came out, carrying an old rocker and some knitting needles and yarn. She put it down in the yard near Holly.

Babs sat down in the chair and began to rock very fast. She put on a huge pair of spectacles and picked up her knitting needles.

Susie dashed across the yard and hastily climbed up a rope ladder into the tree house built in the big oak tree. And Jane, the tailor, clicking a big

40

pair of shears, sat down cross-legged on the ground beside Babs.

Everyone became quiet, and Holly started to read. For a while there was no other sound except the occasional "Whoo—hooting" of Owl Susie up in the tree.

At last Holly came to the part of the story where Mary looks into the pool and sees herself.

Holly stopped reading and closed the book.

"That is the end of the fairy story," she told the mothers with a shy smile. "The story of the fairy Brownie is going to turn into the story of the real Brownies now."

She leaned forward, her eyes sparkling with excitement to watch Karen.

Babs' big sister, Andrea, in a green Girl Scout uniform, stood among the trees back of the lovely little pool by the rock garden. Miss Shay and Mrs. Baker were there with her.

Andrea stepped forward.

"What are you looking for, Karen?" she asked.

"I am looking for a Brownie, like the girl in the story that Holly read," said Karen.

"Let me help you find her," said Andrea. Taking Karen by the shoulders, she turned her around slowly three times. Then Karen knelt down and looked into the pool and Andrea said,

"Twist me and turn me
And show me the Elf,
I looked in the water
And saw ——"

"Myself," sang out Karen, jumping to her feet.

That was the signal for all the other girls to run
to the pool, to be turned about, and to take their
turns looking into the water.

Then Miss Shay came forward.

"Why do you want to be a Brownie, Karen?"
she asked.

"I think because it's such fun and because I
want to learn to do things to help people," said
Karen, stepping up in front of Miss Shay.

Miss Shay leaned down and pinned a Brownie

pin on the right side of the collar of Karen's new uniform.

"I am pinning this Brownie pin on upside down," she said. "After you have done one good turn for someone at home, your mother may turn your trefoil and pin it on right side up."

Then Mrs. Baker stepped forward and stood beside Miss Shay.

"You are a real Brownie now, Karen," she said with a smile. Karen raised her right hand and gave her a snappy salute and a Brownie handshake. The girls all clapped as she stepped back into the ring, and then they took their turns to get their trefoils.

When they had all been invested, the girls stood in a horseshoe and gave the Brownie Promise together. Then they rushed back to show their upside-down pins to their mothers, and to serve the punch and cookies that were on a table on the brick patio.

7.

THE QUARREL

Each girl served her own mother, walking very slowly and using great care not to spill a drop of the punch. Karen carried her cup to Miss Shay. She was standing by Holly, talking to a fat, jolly-looking little man who was standing behind Holly's chair.

"This is my grandfather who has come to visit me," said Holly proudly to Karen.

"I came over to wheel her home," said the man. "I've been watching the goings on from the kitchen window."

"The girls want Holly to become a Brownie,"

said Miss Shay. "They hope she will join their troop soon."

Just then Babs came walking toward them. She was balancing a cup of punch in each hand.

"My mother said to bring this to Holly and her grandfather," she announced. "Then I'll bring a big cupful for me and you, Karen."

"Thank you," said Holly's grandfather. "My, my, this does taste good." He drank his punch and then pushed Holly's chair off in the direction of her house.

46

All the Brownies crowded around to shout and wave good-by, and Holly's eyes glowed like two stars as she waved back.

"Let's get ourselves some punch, and then I'll walk you home, Karen," Babs offered, slipping her arm through Karen's.

A few minutes later, as the two friends started down the walk together, Karen said, "Oh, Babs, don't you just love Holly? And I like her grandfather. You know he seems sort of like a Brownie, too—a grandfather Brownie, I mean." And Karen giggled.

Babs did not answer. She pulled a picture out of her pocket.

"I'm going to win a horse," she said. "Isn't he a beauty? I've always wanted a horse like that—a shiny black one with white feet. I'm in a contest, and I'm going to win him."

"How do you know you are going to win him?" asked Karen.

"Oh, I'm not sure. I have to name this horse. I've sent in ten names already, and I'm trying to think of some more."

"You're always talking about horses, Babs," said

Karen, laughing. "Would you let all the Brownies ride him if you won him?"

Babs frowned. "I am not always talking about horses," she answered crossly. "But you're always talking about Holly. It's Holly this and Holly that. I'm sick and tired of Holly. I thought I was your best friend."

Karen looked at Babs in surprise.

"Of course, I like Holly," she said. "What is wrong with that? Holly is a nice girl. And she's beginning to walk again. She told me so. Pretty soon she'll be a Brownie, too."

"Well, who cares? You always laugh about my horses, and then you talk and talk about Holly. Pretty soon I'm gong to have my own horse. And then you won't make fun of me. And I won't let anyone else ride him either. You can just have Holly Hillman for your best friend. You can go to her house right now if you want to. I'm not going to walk you home."

Babs snapped her mouth shut. She held her head up high and turned around and went up the hill toward her house without looking back even once.

Karen stood still, looking after her, puzzled.

"Now what's the matter with her?" she wondered. "If that is the way she feels, I don't want her for a friend."

Karen walked slowly toward her house. But she was not really mad at Babs. Instead she was unhappy. Only when she came in sight of her own front gate, did her eyes begin to sparkle again.

I can hardly wait to show Mother and Pooky and Mrs. Apple my new pin, she thought. I can hardly wait to think up a good turn to do so I'll get my pin turned the right way.

Suddenly her mind gave a jump.

"Say, that's it," she cried. "Maybe if I do a good turn for Babs and surprise her, maybe she won't be mad at me anymore. Maybe I can win that horse for her if I can think up a good name. I wonder if I could name a horse? Let's see—Goldy—Tiger—Sugarfoot—Firefly—Buttermilk—"

8.

THE BROWNIE SMILE

Karen woke just as the little clock on her dresser chimed eight. The sunshine poured across her bed in a golden stream. It was a glorious day.

"Clothes that peel or tie," chanted Karen to herself. She slipped her jeans on over her shorts, pulled a sweater over her T shirt, and tied a bright red ribbon in her hair.

Down the stairs she raced two at a time and began to gulp the bowl of cereal set for her on the breakfast table.

"Slow down, Karen," said her mother. "What's the rush?"

"I'm a firewood gatherer," said Karen. "I had to collect the firewood for today. Andrea is going along to build our campfire. This will be our very first real campfire. And we are going to cook hot cocoa. Babs has charge of the cocoa pot. Oh, Mother, isn't it exciting?"

"Don't forget your nose bag," reminded Mrs. Grant.

Karen giggled.

"Isn't that a cute name for our lunches, Mother? Nose bags."

She slipped out of her chair as her mother handed her the bag of lunch.

"My firewood and tinder are all stacked in Pooky's wagon so I can pull it to Mrs. Baker's car to be packed. I gathered it all myself yesterday afternoon."

Pooky looked surprised.

"Pooky's wagon!" he exclaimed. He scrambled down from the table and started toward the door, half his piece of toast in his hand.

"Come back, Pooky," shouted Karen. "Oh, please, Pooky. Please let me take your wagon—just this once."

Pooky sat down in the middle of the kitchen floor. He opened his mouth wide and began to howl. Karen looked hopelessly at her mother who reached into a paper bag and quietly put a roll, oozing with jelly and sugar, on the table.

Karen ran over and held the roll above Pooky's nose. His sobs stopped for a moment as he looked at the roll through tear-filled eyes. Then he started howling again, louder than ever.

"Oh, dear," said Karen. She reached into her nose bag and took out three marshmallows which she put on top of the roll.

She set the roll with the marshmallows on top of the breakfast table.

"Look, Pooky," she said. "Some real Brownie marshmallows! Three of them, on top of your roll."

Pooky eyed the marshallows for a moment. His sobs stopped. His chin still quivering, he climbed back on his high chair and reached for the sweets. Karen, seeing her chance, gave her mother a bear hug, planted a noisy kiss on the back of Pooky's head, and was out the door with a bang.

"Have you your warmest sweater on and an extra pair of socks in case your feet get wet?" called Mrs. Grant. But Karen did not answer. Away she went with her load of kindling and firewood rattling over the pavement behind her.

Most of the Brownies were already at the car, and Andrea and Mrs. Baker were packing the supplies into her old station wagon.

Karen pulled her wagon of firewood over to Andrea. Babs was turning somersaults around her big sister and shouting in a loud voice, "Andrea is a Girl Scout. Andrea knows all about building fires and cooking cocoa and making s'mores."

"Hi, Babs," cried Karen.

She ran up to Babs, hoping she had forgotten about being mad.

"Can I be your partner for today, Babs? Can I ride in your station wagon?" Karen asked anxiously.

But before Babs could answer, Andrea spoke.

"Oh, that reminds me," she said. "Line up girls. We are going to draw for partners. I have some colored leaves here in this box. Reach in and draw a leaf. Then match it to get your buddy for the day. Your buddy stays with you when you hike or explore and goes with you in the car both there and back. Yellow or green or orange leaves go in Mrs. Foster's car; red or brown or mixed leaves in Mrs. Baker's station wagon."

Karen drew quickly.

"An oak leaf," she shouted. "Get a red oak leaf, Babs."

But Babs drew a yellow maple leaf.

"I'd rather ride in Mrs. Foster's car than in my

own anyway," shouted Babs and off she ran with her partner. Laughing and giggling they climbed into Mrs. Foster's big white car.

Karen felt tears smarting behind her eyelids.

Babs didn't want to be my partner, she thought. She didn't even say "Ees - u" to me when she ran off.

Just then Susie came running up with a red oak leaf.

"My leaf matches yours, Karen," she said with a happy smile.

"Oh dear," said Karen, frowning. She began to run as fast as she could toward Mrs. Baker's station wagon.

I'm not going to be stuck with that Susie, she thought.

Then she turned and saw Susie still standing there, her eyes timid and troubled behind the big glasses.

Suddenly Karen didn't want to hurt Susie's feelings. She lifted her hand and shouted.

"Hey—hurry up, you're my buddy. Hurry, or you'll get left."

Susie came running as fast as her legs could carry her. Her glasses bumped up and down on her nose as she ran.

She crowded close to Karen who put her arm around her and hugged her tight.

As the motor of Mrs. Baker's station wagon began to whir and hum, the six Brownies in it began to sing at the top of their lungs.

I've something in my pocket
It belongs across my face,
And I keep it very close at hand
In a most convenient place.
I'm sure you couldn't guess it
If you guessed a long, long while.
So I'll take it out and put it on
It's a great big Brownie smile.

9.

FIRST AID FOR BABS

When the two cars arrived at Rockwood, the National Girl Scout Camp, everyone became very busy. A man met the cars, and after they had registered at the Lodge, he led the way along paths flaming with autumn colors, to their picnic place. The Brownies trailed along behind, arms full of bundles and bags and firewood.

"Have a happy time exploring," the man said. "But remember at Rockwood you may not carry things away. Leave the flowers and ferns for others to enjoy, and don't cut or mar the beautiful trees."

After the man had gone, Mrs. Baker said, "An-

58

drea and Mrs. Foster and I will lay the campfire and start it. That will take about half an hour. Go see what surprises you can find in the woods. Stay with your buddy, for you know a Brownie never goes exploring alone. Climb the hills on all sides, but stay within sight of the campfire. When I blow the whistle, it will be time for lunch."

As the girls dashed off in all directions, Mrs. Baker called after them, "No wading in the creek, of course. The water is too cold."

"Maybe we'll meet a horse," shouted Babs, and up the path through the rocks she raced with her buddy. Karen could hear them laughing. What a good time they were having. Karen wished Babs would look back and wave to her. She wished Susie was as much fun to be with as Babs.

"What's in that box, Susie?" she asked curiously as they started up the hill together.

"It's my first-aid box," said Susie proudly. "I have yellow soap in it, in case I get into poison ivy, and some stingy stuff and some cotton and band-aids. My mother is very particular. She always likes me to have a first-aid box when I go on a picnic."

Karen took hold of Susie's hand. "Come on, let's run," she said.

It was a wonderful day. Everything seemed to be moving—the leaves all over the trees were rustling and dancing—the sunshine slid and jumped. The girls ran and skipped.

"Look!"

Susie pointed to a squirrel as he gave a jump from one branch of a tree to another. As the girls watched, he sat back and looked at them with his bright little eyes, and then with a flip of his tail he was gone.

"Yikes," cried Karen bending down. "What a big turtle." She picked him up, and he immediately took his tail, head, and legs indoors.

"Put him down, Karen," begged Susie. "He wants you to. I know he does. Don't hurt him."

As Karen put the turtle down, Jane and her partner raced up.

Jane held something in her hands. It was a huge caterpillar on a leaf.

"Isn't he a big one," she cried.

Susie turned her head away. "I don't like bugs," she said.

Jane laughed.

"Bugs!" she cried. "This isn't a bug, silly, it's a caterpillar and will probably be a beautiful, beautiful butterfly someday."

"Well," said Susie, "I don't like caterpillars, and I don't like bugs, and I don't like snakes. I would probably have a heart attack if I saw a snake."

It was Karen's turn to laugh.

"Oh, Susie," she said, "there aren't any snakes around here, only maybe little garter snakes."

Just then Jane gave a shout and pointed up the path.

"Get down from there, Babs Baker," she cried.

The girls looked. There was Babs, climbing up to the very top of a small sapling. It was bent way down under her weight.

Karen raced up the path.

"Babs Baker, I'm going to tell your mother. You know what that man said about trees. You'll fall and hurt yourself."

"Tattletale," shouted Babs. "Why don't you mind your own business, Karen Grant. The man told us not to break or cut trees, but he didn't say one word about climbing them. Ouch! Now see what you've done."

Babs had started to slide down, and her clothes had caught on a limb. There she stuck, the seat of her jeans ripping every time she moved.

The girls all stood looking up at Babs.

"Well, do something," shouted Babs.

Suddenly Susie put her first-aid kit down on the path.

"I'll help you," she cried. "I'm little. I won't break the tree."

Up she went like a monkey, released the jeans, and slid quickly down.

Babs slid after her.

"Thank you for rescuing me, Susie," she said in a high voice, holding the torn jeans together with one hand. "Now I suppose I'll have to go back and get a safety pin from my mother, and all on account of you, Karen Grant."

"Wait," cried Susie, smiling. Opening her first aid kit, she pulled out a huge safety pin and fastened the torn jeans. Off Babs walked to join her buddy, her head high in the air. Jane and her partner ran off to hunt more caterpillars, and Karen and Susie followed behind.

10.

SUSIE TO THE RESCUE

"Everything I say to Babs makes her madder and madder," said Karen, sadly. "I don't think she'll ever make up with me."

Susie looked at Karen and her face became sad, too.

"Babs sits next to me in school, but all she ever talks about is horses," she declared.

"Can you keep a secret Susie, Brownies honor?" asked Karen.

"Oh, yes, I'm very good at keeping secrets," said Susie.

"Well, I'm trying to win a horse for Babs so

she'll be friends with me again. Do you know any good horse names I could send in to a contest?"

Susie screwed her eyes up tight, thinking. "I don't know anything about horses," she said. "And I don't know any horse names. But maybe Holly does. Holly collects horses. She has a whole shelf full. I saw them one day when my mother stopped by her house to talk to her mother."

"Oh!" exclaimed Karen. "Oh, I didn't know that. I'll ask Holly about horse names. She will know."

The two girls had come to the creek that splashed along through the rocks.

"I wish it wasn't too cold to take off our shoes and go wading," said Karen. "Let's get down on our knees and get a drink."

"Oh, no," said Susie, in a shocked voice. "You'll die if you drink water in the woods, Karen."

The girls sat down on their knees and gazed into the bubbling brook. Suddenly something fell from a nearby tree that bent out over the water. It came floating along down the middle of the stream.

"What is that, Karen?" cried Susie. "Is it a little animal?"

The girls looked closely. It was a little gray bird. It splashed along, beating one wing. The other wing lay spread out limp on top of the water.

"Oh, it's hurt, Karen. Its wing is hurt."

There were tears in Susie's eyes.

The girls watched the bird as it floated by. Suddenly Susie went splashing into the water.

"Susie, you'll get wet," cried Karen. "Come back."

But Susie splashed on. In a moment the bird was cupped in her two hands. Back she came, her jeans soaked to the knees and water squishing out of her sneakers.

"Oh, the poor little thing," said Karen, stroking its back and hanging wing gently as it thrashed about in Susie's hands.

"Let's make it a nest, Karen," cried Susie excitedly. "Get the first-aid box."

Karen unrolled the bandage material and the cotton and made a soft nest. Soon the bird lay in the box between the soap and mercurochrome, its beady little eyes rolling, its hurt wing spread over the band-aids.

A whistle sounded through the frosty air. Susie burst into tears.

"Oh Karen, my feet are all wet and my mother doesn't like me to get my feet wet. Probably I'll catch cold. I'll have to stay out of school. And Mrs. Baker will scold if we bring a bird back with us. I can't go back—what will I do?"

Karen thought a few moments.

"I don't think Mrs. Baker will scold, not when she sees that the bird is hurt, Susie. Come on, don't cry, you can't stay here."

The rest of the girls were all around the camp-fire by the time Susie and Karen got back. Babs and Andrea were stirring the foaming hot cocoa in the cocoa pot. Jane was bending over the pot, too, rubbing her stomach and making hungry noises. They all turned to look as Susie and Karen came slowly down the path. Susie walked behind Karen, carrying her box carefully. Water squished from her soggy shoes and her face was streaked with tears.

"For pity's sake," said Mrs. Baker. "What happened to you, Susie? How did you get all wet?"

Karen put both arms around Susie.

"Please don't scold her," she begged. "Susie got in the water, but she couldn't help it."

"Why, of course I won't scold her," said Mrs. Baker gently. "Come here, Susie, close by the fire. Put on this extra pair of jeans and these socks and sneakers. I thought we might need them, but I never thought they'd be for you."

Mrs. Baker smiled and put out her hand.

"Come Susie, show us what you have in your box."

All the girls came crowding around and there were many "ohs" and "ahs" when they saw the hurt bird. They listened while Karen told how Susie had saved its life.

"May I take it home?" asked Susie. "I couldn't bear to leave it. It might die."

"I'm sure you may take it," said Mrs. Baker comfortingly. "We will ask, but I'm sure no one would want us to leave the hurt bird alone. You will have to watch over it carefully," she warned.

Susie kept the bird right beside her while the girls opened their nose bags and drank their cocoa.

She watched over it while they sat around the campfire and sang songs and ate their fill of s'mores, the Brownie dessert made of graham crackers and chocolate and toasted marshallows.

When the girls played Red Rover and The Elephant Went Out Walking on a Spider's Web, Susie held the box on her lap and tried to feed the bird raisins she had saved from her lunch.

70

"Time to go home," said Mrs. Baker at last.

"I've never had such a good time in my whole life," said Babs, who was always best of anyone at games.

After everything was picked up and clean and the fire had been carefully put out, Karen ran to Mrs. Baker and saluted. All the Brownies lined up behind her.

"Brownie Troop 5 reporting," said Karen.

"Is everything clean?" asked Mrs. Baker.

"Cleaner than we found it," answered Karen.

"Then let's give a cheer for Rockwood and be gone," said Mrs. Baker.

"Rah for Rockwood," shouted all the Brownies.

"Rah for Susie for saving the bird," shouted Karen.

They all raced to the cars and got in.

Susie crowded into the station wagon beside Karen. The bird in the box was more lively and had begun to thrash about.

"Put my handkerchief over him," said Karen. "Mother puts a cloth over our canary bird when she wants him to keep quiet."

Susie gave Karen's arm a squeeze. "I like you

better than any girl in the whole world," she said. "I wish we could have a cook-out every day."

She pressed close to Karen's side. Her soft blue eyes looked up at Karen.

Darling Susie, thought Karen. I love her as much as Holly. Only Babs is mean and cross. If only Babs would be my friend again.

11.

HOLLY FOR CHRISTMAS

Karen was having a talk with her mother. Prayers had been said, and Pooky was fast asleep in his crib. Mrs. Grant sat on the edge of Karen's bed, and the two talked softly together.

"Babs is really mad at me, Mother," said Karen. "She hasn't come to see me for a long time. And she never speaks to me, only in games at recess sometimes. I don't know what to do, Mother. I sent in a lot of horse names to try and win a horse for her. Holly helped me, and Susie helped me. We sent in a hundred names, I guess. But all Babs won was a picture of a horse—a great big picture.

She carries it around everywhere. She shows it to everyone but me. What's the matter with her? What can I do to make her be nice to me again?"

Karen gave an enormous sigh, and looked up at her mother pleadingly.

"If I were you, chick-a-biddy," she said, "I'd just stop thinking about Babs for a while. Christmas is coming you know, and Christmas is a time for every child to help others. Maybe if you and all the Brownies begin thinking hard about how you may be friends to all children everywhere at Christmas time, perhaps you and Babs may become friends again, too. Why don't you try it?" And Mrs. Grant kissed Karen again and turned out the light.

After her mother had gone into the other room, Karen felt better. She lay in the dark for a long time, listening to Pooky's soft breathing and thinking of what her mother had said. And then all of a sudden she had an idea. Smiling, she turned on her pillow and dropped off to sleep.

The next afternoon in Brownie meeting, Karen told her idea.

"I thought of a project for Brownies for Christmas," she told Mrs. Baker. "I thought maybe part of our Brownie project could be Holly."

"Holly and mistletoe?" asked Babs. "Trimming the rec room and stuff like that?"

"Oh, no, I mean Holly Hillman," said Karen, her eyes shining. "Couldn't we have our Christmas meeting at Holly's house, Mrs. Baker? We could take her some things and have a party for her. She has been sick a long time. And it's nice to have a party."

"I saw Holly sitting by the window when I came to Brownies," said Susie. "She waved to me."

"Oh, Mrs. Baker, maybe I could be Santa Claus," shouted Jane. "I was Santa Claus in a Sunday school play, and I still have my suit. I can carry the presents to Holly. No one will know who I am if I wear my Santa Claus mask and beard."

Karen clapped her hands in delight. "Jane would make a good Santa Claus."

"Could I sing a carol for Holly?" asked Susie. "I know 'Silent Night' all by myself."

"Well," said Mrs. Baker. "Usually our Christmas project is for more than one girl. It is something like pasting TB stickers on envelopes for

the Christmas seal drive or making favors for the trays of the children that are in hospitals.

"But we'll think about it. I'll have to talk to Holly's parents of course. That is, if you all want to do it."

All the Brownies shouted "Yes" except Babs.

"I think it would be more fun to take favors to a hospital," she said.

Susie spoke.

"You could see Holly's horses if you went to Holly's house, Babs."

"Oh, yes," cried Karen. "Holly has a whole case full of horses. She collects them. Her grandpa said she used to ride all the time before she got sick."

"Oh," said Babs. She began to look interested.

"What kind of presents shall we take?" asked Jane. "My Santa Claus sack is big. I can carry lots of presents in it."

"Let's give Holly all kinds of things," said Karen excitedly.

"Just a minute," said Mrs. Baker. "We must think of things that don't cost too much. That is the Brownie way, you know."

"Maybe we could make some things," said Jane. "I know how to make hot pads and pen wipers."

"Well," said Mrs. Baker, "suppose we think about it before we meet again. By next week we should all have some wonderful ideas."

Three weeks later the Brownies all crowded around Holly's back door. Big flakes of snow whirled thick and fast outside as Holly's mother opened the door and they crept in. Giggling and whispering they took off their coats and heavy mittens and caps.

"Holly is in the living room," Mrs. Hillman whispered.

The girls tip-toed down the hall and stopped at the living room door. Jane, roly-poly in a red Santa Claus suit, stuck her head in the door. "Ho - ho - ho," she shouted in a squeaky voice. "Merry Christmas—Merry Christmas—ho - ho - ho."

She bounded across the room and dumped a bumpy red sack at Holly's feet. The Brownies followed the fat little Santa, shouting "Merry Christmas—Merry Christmas, Holly."

Karen threw both arms around Holly. "Surprise, Surprise! We're having our Christmas Brownie meeting in your house," she explained. "Isn't that super? And Mrs. Baker says you can open your presents first of all, before we have our meeting. Hurry up, open them!"

Holly, her fingers trembling, reached into the bumpy red bag. "Oh, thank you, Santa Claus Jane," she said, and all the Brownies laughed. Jane pulled off her beard and mask.

"This mask makes me too hot anyway," she giggled. "But how did you guess?"

Miss Shay came in with Holly's mother. "The girls made most of these things themselves," she told Mrs. Hillman, proudly.

Soon Holly was surrounded with rustling white and blue and red tissue paper and piles of gold and silver and green ribbon. With squeals of delight, she held up bookmarks, a clay statue, a book of funny jokes and sayings, and a big red stocking to hang on her front door.

As she got to the bottom of the bag, Susie and Babs ran off into the hall. The rest of the Brownies darted about the room, hanging holly over the windows, setting up a cardboard tree covered with colored gum drop balls, and placing a tiny manger scene on the hearth.

Soon Babs and Susie came back from the hall, carrying two very large, lumpy packages. Susie set her bundle down first. It made strange rustling noises as if something alive was inside it.

Holly pulled off the tissue.

"Oh, Susie," she said. "A little bird—a bird in a cage." She reached in and gathered the bird in her hands. She held it close to her cheek.

"My mom said you would be able to watch it better than me, Holly," said Susie. "Our cat almost ate it the other day while I was at school. I will show you how to feed it and everything you must do to take care of it. And can I please come over to play with it sometimes, Holly?"

There were tears in Susie's eyes.

Karen explained.

"That is the bird Susie found at Rockwood. It's her very special pet. But she wanted to give it to you."

"Oh, Susie, do you really want to give it to me? I'll love having a bird. I'll keep it in my own room and watch it every minute. And of course you can come over to see it every single day if you want to."

Babs still had her arms around her package. She was hugging it tight. When Holly looked up at her, she laid it against Holly's knees, and then walked quickly away. She pretended to watch the fire as Holly pulled off the wrappings. Holly gave a little gasp. It was a painting of a black horse with white feet and a white star on his forehead.

"Babs," cried Holly. "This looks like the horse I used to ride. Oh, isn't it the most gorgeous horse you ever saw? Do you like to ride, too? Oh, when I get better, we'll have to ride together at my grandfather's farm. He has horses, you know."

"Do you really mean it?" asked Babs.

"Of course," said Holly. "And thank you for the picture. I'll hang it over the fireplace. Oh, what wonderful, wonderful Christmas presents."

Babs' freckled face beamed with happiness. She gave a skip, and to Karen's surprise she grabbed her around the waist and whirled her about the room.

"Whoopee," she shouted. "Isn't Christmas fun? I'm so glad you suggested this, Karen."

Oh, thought Karen joyfully. Babs is not mad anymore. No one is mad anymore. It's Christmas, and no one is mad.

12.

SURPRISES

It was a spring day—just one week before school closed. The Brownies were having the last meeting of the year until fall.

Holly's grandfather had invited them to come to his farm. Karen and Babs and Susie were in the Baker station wagon, with Mrs. Baker, Andrea, and Miss Shay. They were rolling along the pleasant countryside toward the farm. Ever since Christmas, Karen and Babs had been friends again.

"Everybody's mother is coming today, Karen," said Susie, "except yours and mine. My mother has a sick headache, and your mother always has to work."

"My mother wanted to come, but she couldn't," said Karen. "She made a luscious chocolate cake for us. She stayed up late last night making it. Isn't it super that Holly's grandfather invited us to his farm for our last meeting and that Holly can be there, too? I haven't seen her for a long time. She's been away."

"You have had an exciting year, haven't you, girls. What have you enjoyed most?" asked Miss Shay.

"The Girl Scout cookie sale last month was fun," said Karen. "I'm glad you sold the most cookies, Babs."

"I liked the Christmas party at Holly's house," said Babs. "What about you, Susie?"

"I think I liked the day at Rockwood," said Susie, "because I found the little starling. Holly is going to bring it to the farm today. She called me up last night and asked me if she could. She is going to let it fly away out of its cage. Its wing is all well, and her grandfather says all wild things should be free in the springtime."

"Here we are," said Mrs. Baker. She turned her car into a narrow side road, and stopped by a little gate. Other cars were parked along the grass. There was a group of tall shade trees and a long picnic table under the trees. Some sleepy-looking cows stood in the sun on a hillside, and at the top of the hill was a white farmhouse and some rambling, red barns.

"Holly's grandfather asked us all to meet him here," explained Mrs. Baker.

Brownies and their mothers were chattering and laughing and moving around the picnic table which was piled high with food. Some of the Brownies were playing a game.

Jane Foster came rushing up to the car.

"Hi Babs, hi Karen, hi Susie," she shouted. "Hurry up. Mom said we can eat as soon as Holly and her grandfather come."

Just then the Hillmans' big black car came rolling down the little side road and stopped close by the gate. Holly was in the back seat of the car.

The Brownies crowded against the fence, waving and calling to Holly. Her grandfather got out of the car first. He came walking across the grass carrying the bird cage. And behind him came Holly. Only Holly was not walking. She was running! She looked brown and happy.

"Oh, Holly," shouted Karen. "When did you learn to walk again? Where have you been for so long?"

"I've been practicing every day," Holly said, smiling. "I've been in Florida with my grandfather. And now the doctor says my leg is almost all right. I am almost well again."

"Can you ride yet, Holly?" asked Babs.

Holly didn't answer, but her grandfather did. "Just wait and see," he said with a laugh.

Grandfather took Holly's arm, and they walked to the picnic table together and sat down.

"Let's eat, everybody," shouted Jane. "It's time to eat now."

She ran to the table and the others followed.

After they had all eaten until they could eat no more, Grandfather turned to Susie.

"Shall we let the little bird try its wings?" he asked.

Susie had taken the cover off the cage and was making little cooing noises to the starling.

Now she lifted the cage and put it in front of Holly. "You open the door, Holly," she said.

All the Brownies gathered around to watch as Holly opened the cage door. But the starling would not come out. It stood there tilting its head from side to side, chirping and looking all about with its beady little eyes.

Finally Holly reached in and took it in her hands. She held it close to her cheek for a moment. Then she put it into Susie's hands.

"Let's carry it out to the gatepost, Susie. Maybe it will fly from there."

Susie carried it lovingly to the fence. She set it down on the broad post.

For a moment the little bird stood there, moving its wings, warming them in the sun.

Then with a flutter, it rose in the air. It flew to a low branch of a nearby tree.

"Maybe it will come back," said Susie. "Maybe it doesn't want to fly and will come back to us."

But suddenly the little bird lifted its wings and spread them wide. Off the branch it flew. Out into the sunshine—higher and higher until it was lost from sight.

The girls watched and watched, even after it was gone. No one wanted to say anything until finally Mr. Hillman said, "Well, who wants to go to the barns?"

"The barns," said Babs excitedly to Karen. "Are we going to the barns?" She began to turn hand-springs down the middle of the path.

The Brownies and their mothers walked slowly over to the sprawling red buildings. They walked through the milking barn—dark and cool with its clean-scrubbed stalls. Then through a smaller barn—smelling of sweet hay. But both barns were deserted.

"The cows and horses are in the pastures," said Mr. Hillman.

On they went out into the sunny meadows. Over the hill some cows were standing, but there was no sign of a horse anywhere.

Then Mr. Hillman put his fingers in his mouth and gave a shrill whistle. From over the curve of the hill two horses came galloping.

One horse went right up to Holly and daintily accepted a lump of sugar from her outstretched palm. It was a black horse with four white feet and a star on his forehead.

"Why, Holly, he looks just like the horse in our picture," cried Babs.

"His name is Star," said Holly.

Mr. Hillman turned to the mothers and Brownies.

"This horse is not just for my granddaughter," he said. "It is for the Brownies—all twelve of them. Holly will be at Hilltop Farm all summer. And I want you to think of Hilltop as the Brownies' summer home. Come out as often as you like. I will be glad to teach any Brownie who wants to learn, how to ride. By the way, is there a Brownie who might like to have a ride right now?"

"Not me," said Susie hastily. "I don't even want to try. I'll just watch."

"I've never had any horse lessons," said Karen. "I think I'll just watch with Susie."

"Me, too," said Jane and all the other Brownies except Babs. They climbed up on the fence and sat in a row with their legs dangling.

Babs walked up to Star. She looked into his thoughtful brown eyes. She ran her hands over his sturdy back.

"Oh, you're beautiful," she whispered.

The horse turned his head and nuzzled her ear gently.

"See, he loves you already, Babs," cried Holly.

Babs looked at her mother and Mrs. Hillman. They were smiling at her and nodding.

"Can I really ride him?" she asked.

"Of course, you can," said Mr. Hillman, coming out of the barn with two, shiny, leather saddles on his arm. "You and Holly can ride together. You can ride Star, and Holly can ride Beauty."

He fastened the cinch of the saddle on Star, straightened the stirrup straps, and handed the reins to Babs.

Babs put her left foot in the stirrup and mounted quickly. Her eyes were glowing with excitement. She clucked to Star, and he broke into a canter.

"Just a minute, young lady," called Mr. Hillman as he fastened the saddle on Beauty and lifted Holly up on the horse. "No racing today. This is Holly's first ride in a long time, you know."

Babs tightened the reins. Star steadied into a trot, and the two horses were off together. Around and around the field they went while the Brownies on the fence shouted and clapped.

"Whoa," cried Grandfather at last. "Slow down. Steady there. It's time to stop."

The two girls pulled up at the fence and Babs
dismounted quickly and gracefully. Mr. Hillman
helped Holly down.

"Thank you Mr. Hillman," Babs cried. "Riding is more fun than anything in the world. Star
is a wonderful horse."

Holly did not say a word. But her eyes glowed
and she did a little skip as she touched the ground.

Mrs. Baker and Miss Shay walked over to the
fence.

"It's time to thank Holly's grandfather for a
lovely day and sing our good night song," Mrs.
Baker said.

So there in the meadow the Brownies made their
circle, while the horses and cows looked on curiously and the mothers gathered round to watch.

94

Karen stood between Babs and Jane. On the other side of the circle, Holly stood between Susie and Andrea.

"Just think," thought Karen, her heart full of happiness. "I just wanted Babs for a friend and no one else. And now I have twelve friends. I guess people need lots and lots of friends."

She squeezed Babs' hand hard as they finished singing, and Babs squeezed back.

Then suddenly Karen clapped her hand over her mouth. "Miss Shay," she cried, looking at her teacher. "Holly is well, and now she can be a Brownie with us. But we'll need a new name. We can't be your Brownie Dozen any more. There will be thirteen of us."

Miss Shay laughed. "Thirteen makes the best dozen of all—thirteen makes a Baker's Dozen.

"Mrs. Baker's Baker's Dozen," shouted Babs as the circle broke up and everyone started to their cars. "What a fabulous name!"

Karen began to run to the station wagon.

"Ees u, Babs," she cried. "Ees u, Susie. Taeb u ot eht rac."

Are you curious about Brownies?

Do you think you might like to become one?

You can join a Brownie Troop if you are seven, eight, or nine years old.

Tell your mother or your teacher at school or your Sunday School teacher, or tell the mother of your friend who is already a Brownie.

Soon you will be invested as a Brownie Scout.

You will wear a Brownie uniform and a cute Brownie beanie. You will have a Brownie trefoil pinned on your collar.

Every week you will go to a Troop meeting.

When you are nine years old you will be ready to "fly up" and become a Tenderfoot Scout. You will change to a green uniform then; and after that you will go on through the ranks until you are a Senior Scout, eighteen years old!

In Brownies, you will make many, many friends for there are one million and 320,000 Brownies in the United States.

What fun they all have—on outdoor hikes and cookouts, exploring the woods, toasting marsh-mallows, sleeping out under the stars, and playing all kinds of fun games. When you are nine years old, you may spend two whole weeks in a camp at the mountains or seashore.

So hurry!

Pack up your nose bag!

Pull on a pair of jeans!

Let's be off adventuring on a Brownie Holiday!